FEATHERS OF FRIENDSHIP

OM PRAKASH KAR

Dedicated to my inspiration,

RUSKIN BOND

Contents

Prologue

Summer came and went in its scorching way, making an everlasting impact on everybody and thus reminding gone were the days of icy cold weather. You could not have found a single person not wandering that the downpours would vanish all the suffering of scorching heat of the summer. But, monsoon didn't go the way everybody anticipated.

Soon, the autumn arrived and everybody was able to ease up a little, thanks to a few occasional showers. The blistering heat lasted for a prolonged period from the month of May up until to the month of October. The heat made its way into every single person mind as the great everlasting heat. The everlasting heat and the disappearance of rain showers had destroyed or rather declined the production of crops, which was one of the major sources of income of hundreds in the village.

A stream of water came pouring down the hill, passing the forest and connecting to a much bigger stream; thus, becoming lifeline for many villagers. At one end, the enormous forest laid flat as far one could see, providing shelter to countless Musk Deer, Black Bear, Tibetan Wolf, Sambar and others yet to be discovered. It went uphill, thus connecting to the Mountain. It was a common sighting of many wild beasts at the river bank as the stream provided a source for them to quench their thirst.

At the other end, lay a huge patch of field meeting an unmetalled road which connected the village with the nearest town.

The field lay uneven with countless tiny peaks, often conquered by myriad hens and cows. At one side where the flow of stream as moderate, some boys had made the land even, thus making it a place for playing their favourite sport – Cricket. While, at the other side laid the uneven patch of field which provided a common area for grazing of cows, from all over the village.

It was time of noon. The sun was at its peak. A frail wind swept across the field, lifting the skirt of a small girl, which she adjusted swiftly. She slept there with her back on a small summit near the bank of the stream.

Due to unforeseen weather, the level of water was low, making it easy for any wild creatures to cross the stream and probably harm her. But, she lay flat there without being agitated of any sudden attack.

She wore an elongated sky blue skirt, which covered her fragile body up from her shoulders to down till her knees. She looked feeble as if a violent breeze would carry her up into the sky, throwing her away a few hundred of miles away. But, she looked firm as she was mentally-strong. She wore a pair of bangles on both her hands. She looked as if she was in his early-teens, probably aging between 14 or 15 years old.

"Hey! Gouri, come here. Maa is calling us." A deafening sound startled her.

She looked behind her. It was a tall, sturdy boy probably in his teens waving hands at her. His bulky arm was bundled with strong muscles, which made him a perfect figure for a weight-lifter or a wrestler. He had short hair and clean cheeks with thin moustache between his nose and lips. He looked sturdy and a person bundled with a lot of responsibility.

Beside him, she saw a middle-aged woman wearing a red sari dotted with various designs. Her face looked as if she was either too old for her age or too young for her age. She had a long silky hair which she adjusted once in a while,

while dusting and washing a few clothes which lay beside her in a tub.

She stood up and called her, “Time to go home. Come, your bhaiya is waiting.” It was none other than her brother and mom.

Gouri stood up and cried out, “Nandi... Chandi, come, let’s go.”

Nandi; a full brown cow with small horns, but sturdy legs and Chandi - a white cow with black dots in some parts, with elongated horns and a symbol similar to crescent moon (Chand) in her forehead.

Both of them came running towards her.

The five of them crossed the field and went towards the village.

The village lay flat in the valley between two mountains, disconnected from the outer world. It was backwards, underdeveloped and often ignored by the government. A narrow road, which went across around one of the summit, connected the village to the nearest town. Nobody knew where the road ended; many rumoured that it connects to a highway and went further to a huge city.

Majority in the village were still involved in primary activities; either agriculture or dairy activities. Thus, the nearest town provided them with various different necessities. A very few people were privileged enough to went further down the road to another town or city in their lifetime.

But, all this did not matter a single bit to Gouri. She was just contented as long as she had her family and company of Nandi and Chandi.

CHAPTER ONE

Feathers of Friendship

"I am going to leave this village. I will found some work in the nearest town." Kishan, Gouri's brother announced while they were having their dinner.

This was too sudden for Gouri. She had never ever imagined her being separated from her brother, even in her wildest dreams. Gouri and her brother were born and raised in this village. They had never left the village.

"Don't go Bhaiya." she replied hastily while being shocked and surprised at the same time.

"I have to go. There is no work left here."

"But, we can still make money with milk from the cow and the vegetables in our field."

"That is not enough. We have to make some more money, or we will perish."

Gouri, Kishan and their mother lived in their small patch of land, which they had inherited from their forefathers. Their house was situated at the centre of patch of land.

It was a small hut made with clay and mud, with its roof covered with bamboo and straws. Regardless, the roof was not as sturdy as Kishan; it leaked from various different areas. Especially, during monsoon their house would be filled with mud as if a flood had just occurred. Kishan was not wrong; they were facing hardships.

The remaining parts of their field served as grazing field for Nandi and Chandi. It was their dining table. Gouri and her mother had used the patch to grow different vegetables. They had planted a few mango trees, which always promised a good source of income for them.

But, the patch of vegetables was not able to produce enough surplus produce for them to sell in the vegetable market that year. Although Gouri would make a staple income by delivering milk to their neighbours each day but, they all knew that it wouldn't be permanent.

"Ever since our father died, we all had been thrown out to poverty." Kishan continued.

"But Bhaiya, you can still make money by working at Sethji's field." Gouri argued.

"No, the produce... is not as good as previous years."

"So... What?"

"Sethji is only a business-minded person. Not that I hate him. But, I'm pretty sure; he won't reduce profits no matter what."

"Bhaiya, what is wrong with that then?" Gouri said, while grabbing Kishan's arms.

"Can't you understand? There is no guarantee of work next season." Kishan screamed in an annoyed way.

Kishan was not mistaken. He used to work at a Seth's field. But, the heat had reduced the produce and it seemed that Seth had managed to make profit this year by reducing the wages of workers. Moreover, there was no guarantee of work next season.

"Maa, at least you explain something to him." Gouri said, while turning back to her mother who was seating in a corner in front of fire making few rotis.

Maa took a glare at Kishan's face and responded, "He is an adult and old enough to take his own decisions."

"Maa...You also..." Gouri said.

"But, remember the year your father died also had a scorching heat, kind of similar as this year. I hope this isn't a bad omen." their mother said, interrupting Gouri.

"Yes, it is a bad omen. Don't leave bhai." Gouri said hastily.

Kishan didn't reply but, instead looked down.

Gouri cried out and left the house. Kishan tried to stop her. But, as he was ready to leave through the main door, his mother stopped her. He stared through the door towards Gouri getting a seat on a pile of rocks and crying silently there.

"Want more roti?" his mother asked, taking her seat near the fire.

"No, I had my fill." Kishan replied.

Gouri sat there alone on the pile of rocks; not because he was waiting for somebody to come and console her as she knew it was only her problem. She knew deep in her heart that her brother had to leave her one day just as any other young adult in her village.

But she was not ready to accept the fact, even though she had seen numerous men from all over the village leaving the town. She herself had imagined travelling far away from this shitty place; to know where that road ended; to have found a new place to settle down. But, all this she dreamt about was with her family, her brother Kishan, her mother, her friends Nandi and Chandi.

As she wandered what had happened, her cries had vanished, leaving her cheeks dry. She probably would had stood up, went to the hand pump in the corner of the shed where Nandi and Chandi slept, but she was not able to do so.

This abrupt realisation made her wander if she would leave the place together with her brother Kishan. But, she knew her brother would complain about her school.

Gouri went to the village school. The village only had a primary and a middle school. Gouri went to the middle school. For further studies, people in the village had either to go to high school in the nearest town or to some unknown city, which only the rich Seth could afford.

He had sent his son way further into city of Kolkata to study in college. There were almost no complaints about sending students to nearest town, except the fact that by foot or cycle it took more than half a day to reach there. Not even a single bus, travelled between the two places. Everybody in the village had accepted their fate.

The village was underdeveloped, except the Seth's three-storey house there was not even a single house which had a concrete roof. You can always find Seth's son brimming over the fact that he was rich enough to afford a cricket kit.

Kishan, unlike Gouri was a very bright student. He firmly believed that study is a pair of wings to gain a successful life. But, regrettably he never got to study further. After the death of his father, he had to give up on his will to acquire those wings and had to work from an early age.

Regretfully, he had never developed the feeling of friendship. He was never able to have any friends. The only friendship he knew of was that of brotherhood.

As Gouri sat there weeping and wandering what to do, she saw a tall boy approaching her. She didn't seem to mind his sudden appearance. That young boy had successfully managed to escape the eyes of Kishan and his mother.

"Hey, your tears are precious. Shed them after you get scolded by your in-laws." A feeble sound reached the ears of Gouri.

Most probably, the boy wanted to make sure nobody is overhearing them. Gouri didn't like the joke much; regardless she grinned a bit and moved his head up to take a good look at the source of sound.

As she looked up concurrently, a gusty wind blew out the creeper hanging over the pile of rocks. It also blew some of her hair and her ponytail became uncombed.

Regardless, she looked up and found boy standing there as an eccentric electric pole.

She looked cautiously at him. He was a tall fellow but, rather thin as if a matchstick. His hands were fragile, unlike her brother, he lacked physical strength. He was wearing a yellow t-shirt and denim trousers.

Gouri recognised this fellow. She had seen him numerous times staring at her from a distance but, never did start a conversation. She became cautious of any potential dangers.

"Could you dare to introduce yourself?" Gouri questioned, while being cautious.

"My introduction could be delayed. What matters is your cry?" the boy said, again in a feeble voice.

"Well, weeping is what left for me. My brother will leave tomorrow. Tell me what I should do?"

"Do anything except crying."

"Maa is okay with Bhaiya leaving. Bhaiya would probably be happy too. Only I am the problem."

"They are not happy; they have just accepted the truth."

"How could you say so when you don't even know what problem I'm currently having?"

"I know." he said, took a brief pause and continued, "I know. When I lost my parents, the ones dearest to me, I wept a lot, I cried a lot. But, what happened? Was I able to bring back my parents?"

"Then, what did you did?"

"I moved on."

"Does it help to change the problem?"

"No! But, it makes you happy. And, the sole purpose of our existence is to find happiness."

Gouri remained silent .The boy turned around and was ready to depart. But, he turned around, waved at her and screamed out, "Remember this! No matter whatever happens, be happy."

Gouri stood up as she realised the boy was leaving. Not knowing what to say she cried out, "What is your name?"

"It's Keshav." Saying this, the boy vanished into the dark.

Gouri went home afterwards and slept in her cot, without speaking a word.

As soon as the dawn vanished all the darkness, his brother was ready to depart on his journey. His mother was there at the door.

"Gouri is still angry with me, maybe I should not leave after all." Kishan said to his mother.

As soon as Kishan said this, Gouri appeared from behind her mother and said, "Bhai, You forgot your towel."

"Don't just go with forgetting things." Gouri said while putting the towel inside Kishan's bag.

"Gouri, you, but..." Kishan said, while being startled.

"No ifs and buts. Just go already, you might get late or do you want to get hunted down by some wild beasts on the way there?" Gouri said pushing Kishan towards his cycle.

Kishan rode his bicycle, pedalled it with maximum force and went on his way. Gouri waved at him as far he could see him.

Soon, the sun was high up in the sky, reminding everybody to get to their work. Shops were opening, farmers were getting ready to get to their field, labourers were wandering where they had to work today, poultry animals became alive and others probably still dozing in their beds. The village had become alive in a matter of few minutes.

The School was closed that day, that's the reason why children in enormous quantity could be seen either playing cricket or soccer, while the younger ones gazed at the elders hitting huge sixes or making an eccentric goal.

Gouri had a day off from school. Usually she used these days to fetch milk from cows and dispense milk to their neighbours; thus earning a part-time gig. However, today she had put off this job of her mother, who didn't seemed to complain either way.

As Gouri was wandering how to relish this sublime day of her life, she thought to depart to her favourite place near the stream and to doze in front of the stream.

Routinely, she would have had left with her companions - Nandi and Chandi, but she didn't. She was already half way there, when she realised the absence of both her companions and she was slothful enough not to walk back half way. Thus, she decided for today, she would wander off on her own.

Gouri arrived there swiftly, noticed a few boys had made themselves comfortable under a banyan tree, wandered about the reason and decided to go towards that direction.

The tree seemed enormous, with its branches spreading across all directions. Once in a while, a fragile wind would make the tree shed a few tears in form of leaves. Something seemed marvellous about that tree to Gouri. It attracted Gouri towards that direction as a magnet.

As soon as she made an appearance there, she realised that she had arrived at the other end of the field, where numerous older boys were playing cricket. She took a look towards the banyan tree, grasped that those were older boys from the village eagerly waiting for their turn to field.

Gouri recalled Kishan's advice not to be friendly with them and distanced herself from them.

As Gouri was ready to depart from the scene, concurrently she heard the boys under the banyan tree yelling, "Keshav... Keshav... Keshav..."

Gouri turned around to take a look. She gazed at the boys yelling and screaming.

One boy shouted, "Come on, Keshav. Show them what we have got! Get the revenge for my nose. Come on, Keshav!"

Another boy standing beside him, screamed loud enough to make everyone near him deaf. "Hit a boundary on the last ball."

Everyone screamed together, "Hit a Six... Hit a Six..."

Gouri tried to gaze at the batsman on crease, but unfortunately couldn't. The sun by now had reached its peak.

Gouri put a hand over her eyebrows and again tried to comprehend the batsman.

She looked at his complex physique, tall but thin and then to his face. It was none other than Keshav standing on the crease holding the bat in both of his hands.

As soon as she recognised it was Keshav who was batting she screamed out, "Keshav, hit a six."

Though, she didn't had anything in particular relations to the team, still she was now favouring the batting team.

Gouri's high-pitched and shrill voice reached the ears of Keshav. He was able to differentiate between the voice of a boy and a girl.

He was bewildered after hearing a girl's voice. He tried to look around the ground to search for the source of sound.

He detected it was none other than Gouri screaming for her, who had by now reached the area behind the bowler's back. She stood straight to Keshav.

The captain of the other team came forward to the bowler and whispered, "This is the last ball. His height is helping him to hit short balls, so don't bowl those."

"Then, what should I bowl?" the bowler responded after being confused.

"Bowl a Yorker, not a wide one or into his legs. Bowl a Yorker between the space between his bat and legs. Okay?"

The bowler nodded in approval.

The bowler took a long and speedy run-up, came closer to the pitch and bowled as he was directed.

Keshav was startled when he realised the length and line of the ball, regardless he swung his bat up as it went down hitting the ball, launching straight above the bowler's head straight towards the boundary.

It didn't go towards long off or long on, instead went straight towards where Gouri stood.

Gouri realised the ball approaching her, she raised her hands upwards, jumped and took a magnificent catch, which would probably made her win 'THE PERFECT CATCH OF THE MATCH' award.

Everybody was amazed how Gouri was able to take up a catch.

"Hey, come here!" A loud shrill sound reached the ears of Gouri.

He looked; it was Keshav calling her standing among the boys under the banyan tree. Gouri ran towards Keshav.

As Gouri approached the scene, she was attacked with the question from one of the boys standing beside Keshav, "Can you field?"

"Hey, don't just startle her by asking questions so suddenly." Keshav interrupted. "Okay. Guys, this is Gouri."

"What happened?" Gouri asked.

"Nothing Much... But, do you know rules of cricket?"

"I do. But, before that I want to talk to you."

Gouri had always wondered how cricket was played and persuaded Kishan to teach her to play.

"Can you save the talking to later? I saw how you were able to catch the ball. Can you do that again?"

"Well, my brother taught me. But what happened?"

"Actually, we don't have enough players."

"But, you do have 11 players here."

"Oh! Siddharth here injured his nose while batting. That's why, we need one extra player." Kishan said pointing his hand towards a boy sitting under the banyan tree.

The boy waved his hand at her. She waved her hand at her with an awkward face.

"Do you know every rule?" the boy questioned in a doubtful way.

"Don't worry I know. I can field too." Gouri assured them.

"Then, it is decided. Gouri will be your substitute for today." Keshav announced to his team.

Keshav's team had scored only 107 runs in 20 overs. It was a low score for 20 overs match.

Innings proceeded. Opening pair of the other team was able to make a pretty good score. They didn't hit any big boundaries, instead focused on short singles.

So, Keshav proposed Gouri to be removed from slip position and placed in silly mid on to save up some singles.

After a few overs, three wickets fell down. Though, Gouri was not able to contribute much, she wasn't removed from her position. Probably, Keshav thought this would put some pressure on the other team.

Keshav came to bowl. His first two balls spun rapidly and the batsman was not even able to touch it. But, on the third ball, ball slipped from his hands and batsmen took the opportunity to flick the ball.

The ball rolled down the short grass towards Gouri. She swiftly picked it up, but in confusion threw the ball towards the bowler's end instead. She missed the platinum opportunity of run out.

Keshav shouted, "Don't mind."

But, others remained silent and only glared at Gouri.

Innings proceeded further and last over approached. The opponent team had to hit 11 runs in 6 balls to win the match.

Nobody was ready to take the pressure and bowl last over. Keshav seemed helpless. He took a look at Gouri and threw the ball towards her.

"Gouri will bowl the last over." he cried out.

Three of his team members came forward to complain, but Keshav made them stop by asking them if they want to bowl, they can.

Gouri bowled the first ball; the batsman hit it off on the off side. It bounced on soft grass a couple of times before crossing the boundary. Four!

Everybody looked hopeless.

For the second ball, Gouri took a short run up and threw the ball with maximum force, it bounced half way on the pitch. The batsman swung his bat hard, but missed the ball instead hit the air. The ball went forward and struck the stumps made from branches, flying them a foot away. It was the last wicket.

Keshav's team has won the match and it all because of Gouri. From that day onwards, Gouri became an official member of the team.

The celebration was over, the treat for Gouri had been done for, and now both of them were walking beside a canal as Keshav had promised her to walk her home. To the right side of them laid endless field dotted with crops, which both of them were unknown about. To the left, laid a small canal where younger children were bathing in the fetid waters which flowed leisurely. But all this was inconsequential. All that mattered was both of them wanted to initiate a conversation but, were too shy to do so.

"Um...We didn't get time to talk?" Gouri said. It startled Keshav who was walking beside her.

He responded, "Eh... Yeah! Due to the excitement of winning the match I completely forgot that we were total strangers up until Yesterday." He giggled a little.

"Actually, now that I realise, I don't know a word about you."

"What happened yesterday was... Um..." Keshav said. "Oh. Sorry. Yesterday, I probably spoke a few words I shouldn't."

"No no. Don't be sorry. It was my problem. You just helped me."

They remained silent, walked for a few minutes, and then Gouri said, "So, What do you do?"

"Well, I own a shop. A grocery one. I inherited from my father when he... Um you know what?"

"Oh. I am sorry. I shouldn't have questioned you."

"No, no, no. Don't be sorry. It's alright. Truth is always the truth, right?" he smirked.

Gouri burst out laughing, "What was that? You are just stating the obvious."

"Okay okay, sorry for being such a bad philosopher." Keshav continued, "Now stop laughing."

"Okay-okay, just a second... Now, do you tell me if you own a grocery shop, why you were playing cricket today?"

"Well, I had a day off today. I am still 19. I am allowed to play, okay?"

And they talked all the way to Gouri's home.

Gouri had discovered something unfamiliar today. She had discovered a new feeling for him. Something which was quite different from the relationship she shares with Kishan.

She had for first time in her life discovered friendship.

Printed by Libri Plureos GmbH in Hamburg,
Germany